THE BUMPER BOOK OF
ELMER

First published in Great Britain in 1998 by
Andersen Press Ltd., 20 Vauxhall Bridge Road, London SW1V 2SA.
Published in Australia by Random House Australia Pty.,
20 Alfred Street, Milsons Point, Sydney, NSW 2061. All rights reserved.
Printed and bound in Italy by Grafiche AZ, Verona.

10   9   8   7   6   5   4   3   2   1

British Library Cataloguing in Publication Data available.

ISBN 0 86264 418 6

This book has been printed on acid-free paper

THE BUMPER BOOK OF
ELMER

David McKee

contents

ELMER

ELMER AGAIN

ELMER ON STILTS

ELMER AND WILBUR

Andersen Press • London

ELMER

for Brett

There was once a herd of elephants. Elephants young, elephants old, elephants tall or fat or thin. Elephants like this, that or the other, all different but all happy and all the same colour. All that is except Elmer.

Elmer was different.
Elmer was patchwork.
Elmer was yellow
          and orange
          and red
          and pink
          and purple
          and blue
          and green
          and black
          and white.
Elmer was *not* elephant colour.

It was Elmer who kept the elephants happy.
Sometimes he joked with the other elephants,
sometimes they joked with him. But if there
was even a little smile, it was usually Elmer
who started it.

One night Elmer couldn't sleep for thinking and the think that he was thinking was that he was tired of being different. "Whoever heard of a patchwork elephant?" he thought. "No wonder they laugh at me." In the morning before the others were really awake, Elmer slipped quietly away, unnoticed.

As he walked through the jungle Elmer met other animals.

They always said: "Good morning, Elmer." Each
time Elmer smiled and said: "Good morning."

After a long walk Elmer found what he
was looking for – a large bush. A large
bush covered with berries, a large bush
covered with elephant-coloured berries.
Elmer caught hold of the bush and shook
it and shook it so that the berries fell on
the ground.

Once the ground was covered in berries Elmer lay down and rolled over and over this way and that way and back again. Then he picked up bunches of berries and rubbed himself all over covering himself with berry juice until there wasn't a sign of any yellow, or orange, or red, or pink, or purple, or blue, or green, or black, or white. When he had finished Elmer looked like any other elephant.

After that Elmer set off back to the herd. On the way he passed the other animals again.

This time each one said to him: "Good morning, elephant." And each time Elmer smiled and said: "Good morning," pleased that he wasn't recognised.

When Elmer rejoined the other elephants they were all standing quietly. None of them noticed Elmer as he worked his way to the middle of the herd.

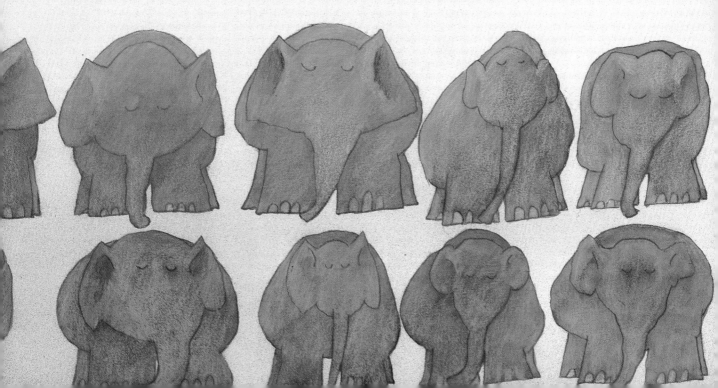

After a while Elmer felt that something was wrong. But what? He looked around: same old jungle, same old bright sky, same old rain cloud that came over from time to time and lastly same old elephants. Elmer looked at them.

The elephants were standing absolutely still. Elmer had never seen them so serious before. The more he looked at the serious, silent, still, standing elephants, the more he

wanted to laugh. Finally he could bear it no longer. He lifted his trunk and at the top of his voice shouted:

The elephants jumped and fell all ways in surprise. "Oh
my gosh and golly!" they said and then saw Elmer helpless
with laughter.

"Elmer," they said. "It must be Elmer." Then the other elephants laughed too as they had never laughed before.

As they laughed the rain cloud burst and when the rain fell on Elmer his patchwork started to show again. The elephants still laughed as Elmer was washed back to normal. "Oh Elmer," gasped an old elephant. "You've played some good jokes but this has been the biggest laugh of all. It didn't take you long to show your true colours."

"We must celebrate this day every year," said another. "This will be Elmer's day. All elephants must decorate themselves and Elmer will decorate himself elephant colour."

That is exactly what the elephants do. On one day a year they decorate themselves and parade. On that day if you happen to see an elephant ordinary elephant colour you will know it must be Elmer.

ELMER AGAIN

Elmer, the patchwork elephant, was bored. It was two days before another Elmer's day parade – the day when elephants cover themselves with bright patterns. The colours were ready and the elephants were quietly thinking about how they would decorate themselves.

Elmer didn't have to think. He was always coloured grey for the parade, the only grey elephant.

"Time for a walk," he said to himself.

As he walked Elmer thought, "It's too quiet
around here. We need a joke or something to liven
things up." He came to a pool and looked at his
reflection.

"Hello Elmer," he said to himself in the water.
"You've just given me a good idea. Thank you."

When he returned the others were still quietly thinking. Elmer went up to one of them and whispered in his ear. The other elephant smiled and winked but said nothing. Elmer settled down for a rest. He had a long night in front of him.

When night fell Elmer waited until the others were asleep.
Then, taking care not to wake them, he set to work.

Before sunrise he had finished and he tiptoed off to another part of the forest to sleep for what was left of the night.

In the morning the first elephant to wake looked at his neighbour and said, "Good morning Elmer."

One after another the elephants woke, and as they did, from every direction came, "Good morning Elmer," "GOOD morning Elmer," "Good MORNING Elmer," "GOOD MORNING Elmer," "Good Morning ELMER," and so on.

During the night Elmer had painted all the elephants to look like him. Now there were Elmers everywhere and nobody knew which was the real one.

Then the elephants started to speak to each other and say things like, "Are you Elmer?"

"I don't know," the other might say. I might be today, but I'm sure I wasn't yesterday."

Then, one of the elephants called out, "This is another Elmer trick. Come on. Let's splash across the river and wash off the colours. Then we'll see who the real Elmer is."

The elephants raced to the river and splashed and sploshed their way to the other side.

Once on the other side the elephants stared. They were *all* grey.

"Where's Elmer?" they asked.

"Here of course," said a grey elephant. "Don't you recognise me?"

"But you're the same colour as us," gasped the others.

"So I am," said Elmer. "Wonderful. I always wanted to be like you."

"This is awful," said another elephant. "Elmer can't be like the rest of us. Things won't be the same without an Elmer."

"Well there's nothing I can do about it," said Elmer, "unless . . ."

"What?" said the others.

"Well," said Elmer, "the colours that washed off are still floating on the water. Perhaps if I run back through them I may return to normal."

"Try it," shouted the others. "Try anything to get your colours back."

"Yahoo!" called Elmer, and he raced across the river and vanished into the trees on the other side.

Almost at once he reappeared puffing and panting,
but once again in his bright patchwork colours.

"Hurrah!" cheered the elephants from across the
river. "It worked. We've got our Elmer again." With
that the elephants started chanting, "ELMER, ELMER,
ELMER."

Beside Elmer another elephant suddenly appeared from out of the trees. "Did you call?" he asked. The other elephants went silent and stared. This other elephant was soaking wet as if he had just run across the river. On top of that both Elmer and the other elephant were laughing.

"You tricked us," said one elephant to the wet, grey elephant. "You were working with Elmer and pretended to be him. We should have known Elmer's colours wouldn't wash off. It's another Elmer trick."

With that the whole herd of elephants burst out
laughing, and running back into the river they started
to splash the two Elmers and each other and once

again they chanted, "ELMER, ELMER, ELMER,"
until the whole jungle shook with their noisy game.

ELMER ON STILTS

One morning, Elmer, the patchwork elephant, met some of his friends. They were looking very worried.

"Oh dear, Elmer," they said. "Those awful elephant hunters are coming. What can we do to escape them?"

"Hmmmm!" said Elmer. "Let me have a think. I'm sure I can come up with something."

Elmer went for a thinking walk. He was thinking about how hunters look for elephant footprints and follow them until they find the elephants when suddenly a voice said,

"Look out, Elmer. Watch where you're going." A very tall giraffe was speaking to him.

"Sorry," said Elmer. "I didn't see you up there. But you've just given me a very good idea," and he hurried off to find the other elephants.

"I've an idea," said Elmer to the others. "Let's walk around on stilts."

"This is no time for jokes, Elmer," said an elephant. "The hunters are coming."

"I'm serious," said Elmer. "Hunters look for us by following our footprints. They'd never look up and see us."

The elephants thought that Elmer's idea was a good one and were soon hard at work. Some made stilts from very strong wood.

Other elephants brought tree trunks and made a ramp
that the elephants could walk up to get onto the stilts.

Elmer went first. He walked up the ramp, and using his front legs to hold on he put his back legs onto the stilts. "It's easy," he called. "My trunk helps me to keep my balance."

Unfortunately, because Elmer was so heavy the stilts immediately sank into the ground.

"Oh no," groaned the elephants. "It won't work."

"I know," said Elmer. "If we put flat pieces of wood on the bottom of the poles, the stilts won't sink into the ground."

"Then if we colour the stilts green," continued Elmer, "the hunters will think they are plants. We can shape the flat bits like monsters' feet. If we put them on backwards, as we walk it will look like a monsters' trail, but going in the opposite direction. The hunters will follow the footprints away from us to try and find the monsters."

It wasn't long before the elephants
were walking on stilts leaving a trail of
prints pointing away from them.
"The more the hunters look, the further
they will get away from us," chuckled Elmer.

There was one thing, however, that Elmer had forgotten. Elephant hunters are cowards. When they saw the footprints, the hunters all said the same thing.

"Oh no, monsters!" Then, shaking with fear, they hurried off in the opposite direction – towards the elephants and . . .

. . . CRASH!
They didn't notice the stilts and bumped right into them.

The elephants fell off, but, instead of falling onto the
hard ground, they fell onto the soft, round, fat hunters.

One by one, Elmer and the elephants got up and walked away. "Dear, oh dear," they said.

It was a long time before the hunters managed to crawl away, moaning. They would never come back.

"Hurrah for Elmer," shouted the elephants. "His idea saved us. Now we don't need the stilts any more."

"We don't NEED them," smiled Elmer. "But we could have some fun on them." And that's exactly what they did.

ELMER AND WILBUR

Elmer, the patchwork elephant, was
waiting for his cousin, Wilbur, who was
coming to visit him.

"He's late," said Elmer. "Perhaps he's
lost. Let's go and look for him."

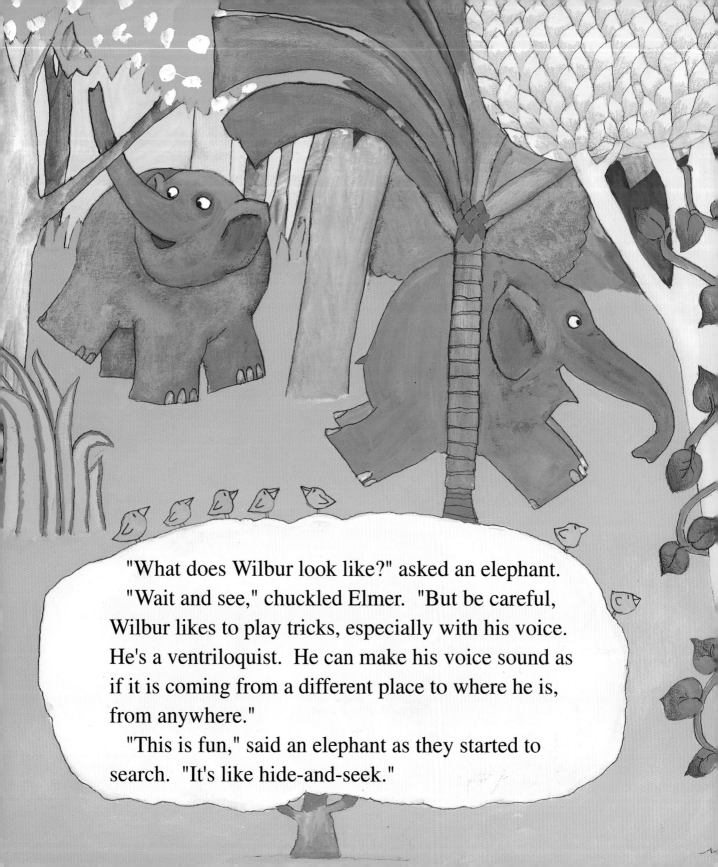

"What does Wilbur look like?" asked an elephant.

"Wait and see," chuckled Elmer. "But be careful, Wilbur likes to play tricks, especially with his voice. He's a ventriloquist. He can make his voice sound as if it is coming from a different place to where he is, from anywhere."

"This is fun," said an elephant as they started to search. "It's like hide-and-seek."

Suddenly they heard, "Yo Ho! Elmer! I'm over here."
They rushed to where the voice came from.
"Looking for me?" asked a rather surprised tiger.
"Sorry," said Elmer, "we thought you were my cousin."
"Very funny, Elmer," said the tiger. "Perhaps that's
your cousin I can hear shouting."

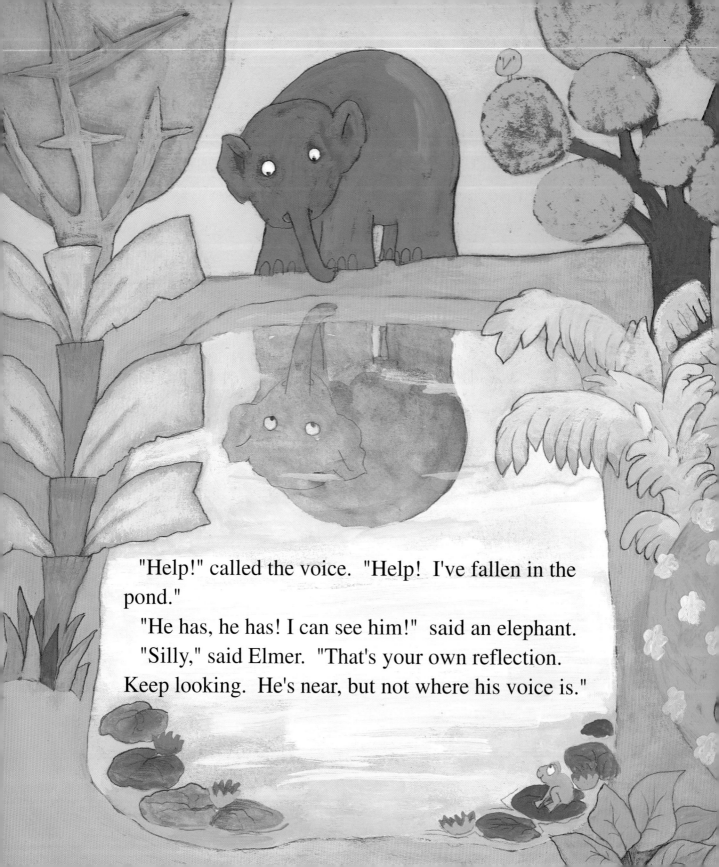

"Help!" called the voice. "Help! I've fallen in the pond."

"He has, he has! I can see him!" said an elephant.

"Silly," said Elmer. "That's your own reflection. Keep looking. He's near, but not where his voice is."

They kept looking and all the time they looked, the voice came from different places. It called, "COOEEE! Here I am," or "BOO!" to make them jump. It even came from down a rabbit hole. The rabbits popped out saying, "That's not funny. That's not funny at all. That's very silly."

After a lot of searching, an elephant said, "We'll never find him, Elmer. Let's give in."

"Wilbur," called Elmer. "We give in. You can come out now."

"I can't. I'm stuck up a tree," Wilbur's voice said from above them. The elephants giggled. "He's very clever," said one.

"If you don't come," said Elmer, "we'll have to go home without you."

"I really am stuck up a tree," said Wilbur's voice. The elephants giggled again.

"Elmer," said an elephant. "Is Wilbur black and white?"

"Yes. Why?" said Elmer.

"I peeped," said the elephant. "He really is stuck up a tree."

They all looked. There was Wilbur, up a tree.
"Wilbur," gasped Elmer. "How did you get up there?"
"Never mind how I got up, how do I get down?"
said Wilbur.

"I've no idea," said Elmer. "But we're hungry so we're going home for tea. At least we know where you are now. Goodbye, Wilbur. See you tomorrow."

With that Elmer started to lead the other elephants away.
"Oh, Elmer," called Wilbur. "Don't leave me. I'm starving."

"Ha, ha, I was just teasing," laughed Elmer, turning back to Wilbur. "If you walk along the branch it will bend down with your weight and we can help you down."

Wilbur walked slowly along the branch. The branch began to bend down. When the elephants could reach, they pulled the branch the rest of the way and helped Wilbur off.

"Thanks," said Wilbur. "Now, where's that tea you were talking about?" Then laughing and joking together they raced all the way home.

That night, as they lay down to sleep, Elmer said, "Goodnight, Wilbur. Goodnight, Moon." A voice that seemed to come from the moon said, "Goodnight, elephants. Sweet dreams."

Elmer smiled and whispered, "Wilbur, how DID you get up that tree?" But Wilbur was already asleep.